Little Red Toopy

Text and Illustrations: Dominique Jolin
English Text: Karen Simon

"Today it's your turn
to be the Big Bad Wolf,"
Toopy tells Binoo.

"Good morning, Mr. Wolf,"
says Toopy.

"What **big** ears you have… The better to hear me with, right?"

"And what **long** arms you have... The better to tickle me with, I suppose."

"And what a **big** smile you have… But it's not 'cause you want to eat me, is it?"

"Oh! You really look like a big bad wolf…"

"And what **big** teeth you have... Now you *can* eat me!!!"

"Help! Help!
The Big Bad Wolf is going
to eat me up!" cries Little Red
Toopy. Little Red Toopy runs
and runs…

… but the Big Bad Wolf has fallen asleep.
"**Wake up**, Mr. Wolf. You're supposed to eat me now!
Wake up **Binoo!**"

**Big Bad Binoo can hear Toopy.
Suddenly he opens his eyes,
pounces on Little Red Toopy
and eats him!!!**

Toopy likes playing the
Big Bad Wolf with Binoo.

Library and Archives Canada
Cataloguing in Publication

Jolin, Dominique, 1964-
[Petit Toupie rouge. English]
Little Red Toopy
(Little Hands)
Translation of: Le petit Toupie rouge.
For children.

ISBN-13: 978-1-55389-012-6
ISBN-10: 1-55389-012-4
I. Simon, Karen. II. Title. III. Title:
Petit Toupie rouge. English. IV. Series: Jolin,
Dominique, 1964- . Little Hands.
PS8569.O399P4713 2006 jc843'.54 C2006-940572-7
PS9569.O399P4713 2006

www.dominiqueetcompagnie.com
Picture Books Collection Director: Lucie Papineau
Artistic and Graphic Direction: Primeau & Barey
Toopy and Binoo typeface design: Primeau & Barey
Copyright: 3rd Quarter 2006

Printed in China
10 9 8 7 6 5 4 3 2 1

We acknowledge the support of the Canada Council
for the Arts for our publishing program.

We acknowledge the financial support of the
Government of Canada through the Book Publishing
Industry Development Program (BPIDP) for our
publishing activities.

Government of Quebec–Publishing Program and
Tax Credit Program–Gestion SODEC